# Grandad's Tree

## Poems about Families

In loving memory of William O. Bulger and his many grandchildren — J. C.
For all my indian family, especially Triambika, Kartiki and Mushahid — J. B.

Barefoot Books
124 Walcot Street
Bath BA1 5BG

This book was typeset in Della Robbia 12pt, Goudy Handtooled 26pt and
ITC Legacy Sans Book
The illustrations were prepared in watercolour

Graphic design by Ben England
Colour separation by Grafiscan, Verona
Printed and bound in Singapore by Tien Wah Press (Pte) Ltd

This book has been printed on 100% acid-free paper

Hardback ISBN 1-84148-540-3

British Cataloguing-in-Publication Data: a catalogue record for this book is
available from the British Library

1 3 5 7 9 8 6 4 2

# Grandad's Tree

## Poems about Families

compiled by **Jill Bennett**

illustrated by **Julia Cairns**

**Barefoot Books**
*Celebrating Art and Story*

# Contents

Introduction 6

What is a family? 8
Mary Ann Hoberman

Mum is Wow! 10
Julia Fields

Dad 11
Berlie Doherty

Mama 12
Lynn Joseph

Missing Mama 13
Eloise Greenfield

My Father 14
Mary Ann Hoberman

In Both the Families 15
Arnold Adoff

Mother Doesn't Want a Dog 16
Judith Viorst

Sauce 18
Pauline Stewart

Our Baby 19
Joan Poulson

Always Remembering Eloise　　　　20
Lindsay MacRae

Sometimes　　　　21
Eve Merriam

The Runaway　　　　22
Bobby Katz

Granny Granny Please Comb my Hair　　　　24
Grace Nichols

Grandpa　　　　25
Berlie Doherty

Let's Be Merry　　　　26
Christina Rossetti

Two Sisters　　　　27
Nancy Wood

Grandad's Tree　　　　28
Rowena Sommerville

Newcomers　　　　30
Michael Rosen

Family　　　　31
Carl Sandburg

Acknowledgements　　　　32

# INTRODUCTION

The word family conjures up many different images and arouses all manner of feelings and emotions, often very deep ones. Not all aspects of family life are happy even in the most secure family units and every family is different. Many children live with only one parent, some are part of an extended family with mum, dad and grandparents living under the same roof, perhaps even aunts, uncles and cousins.

There are small families and large families, and we know that much of what young children learn is rooted in their family life experiences. In this collection I have tried to reflect something of the diversity of families, to look at a range of family members and characters from a child's perspective, and to explore some of the emotions and feelings experienced as part and parcel of family life.

One of my strongest beliefs as a teacher has always been the importance of literature in the education of the imagination: 'what if...or suppose that...', and how poetry in particular can encapsulate whole worlds, micro-worlds, so that a child reading a poem can almost hold that world in his or her hands, examine it, assimilate it and perhaps find a new way of seeing, of knowing, and even of being. Of all literature, poetry offers that potent magic that can be evoked again and again. As Grigson says, 'Poetry comes from playing the best game of words which has ever been invented...it is ideal to fit (the words) into patterns of sound and meaning, each of which, by its rhythm, does not easily wear out and will bear, and insist upon, being read again and again.'

The poems I have chosen are some of those which, when shared with children, have invoked that 'please can we hear it again' response.

One of the vital ingredients of family life is humour, and Mary Ann Hoberman's light-hearted 'What is a family?' introduces a whole host of possibilities. Likewise 'Mother Doesn't Want a Dog' by Judith Viorst allows us to see the humorous side of a family disagreement, and the cleverness of a child's response to her mother's anxiety about adopting a family pet.

The light touch of Lindsay MacRae enables readers to confront one of the saddest facets of family life — loss — in 'Always Remembering Eloise', her memorial to a 'might-have-been' baby. Similarly, Eloise Greenfield in 'Missing Mama' reveals another face of loss — the death of a mother — and depicts the comfort and strength that comes from the community of family which is left behind.

Other aspects of separation are explored in Michael Rosen's 'Newcomers', and Rowena Sommerville's 'Grandad's Tree', both of which remind us of the importance of continuity and how a grandfather's jacket and part of a family garden can become the focus of treasured memories.

I hope some of these poems will also become treasured memories.

Jill Bennett

# What is a family?

What is a family?
Who is a family?
One and another makes two is a family!
Baby and father and mother: a family!
Parents and sister and brother: a family!

*All kinds of people can make up a family*
*All kinds of mixtures can make up a family*

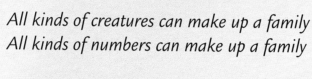

What is a family?
Who is a family?
The children that lived in a shoe is a family!
A pair like a kanga and roo is a family!
A calf and a cow that go moo is a family!

*All kinds of creatures can make up a family*
*All kinds of numbers can make up a family*

What is a family?
Who is a family?
Either a lot or a few is a family;
But whether there's ten or there's two in *your* family,
All of your family plus you is a family!

*Mary Ann Hoberman*

# Mum is Wow!

Mothers are finders and keepers
They are comforters of weepers
They are luller-abye for sleepers.

Mothers are good-manners makers
They are temperature takers
They are the best of birthday bakers.
Mum is Wow!

Mothers are sick-bed sit besiders
They are hiding place providers
They are pin-the-tail guiders.

Mothers are prayer makers in the nights
They are enders of quarrels and fights
They are teachers of duties and rights.
Mum is Wow!

*Julia Fields*

# Dad

Dad is the dancing man,
The laughing-bear, the prickle-chin,
The tickle-fingers, jungle-roars,
Bucking bronco, rocking-horse,
The helicopter roundabout,
The beat-the-wind at swing-and-shot,
Goal-post, scary-ghost,
Climbing-Jack, humpty-back.

But sometimes he's
A go-away-please!
A snorey-snarl, a sprawly lump,

And I'm a kite without a string
Waiting for Dad to dance again.

*Berlie Doherty*

11

# Mama

Mama gone to market
with the figs upon her head.
She wearin' her soft blue
dress for selling
with the fish 'round the hem.
Her hair is plaited neatly
in two long straps of black.
She walkin' tall in sandals
with the bamboo beads intact.
Mama look like Christmas
with red sorrel behind her ears.
She balance her wicker basket
like the star of Bethlehem.

*Lynn Joseph*

12

# Missing Mama

last year when mum died
I went to my room to hide
from the hurt
I closed my door
wasn't going to come out
no more, never
but my uncle he said
you going to get past
this pain
      You going to
push on past this pain
and one of these days
you going to feel like
yourself again
I don't miss a day
remembering Mama
sometimes I cry
but mostly
I think about
the good things
now

*Eloise Greenfield*

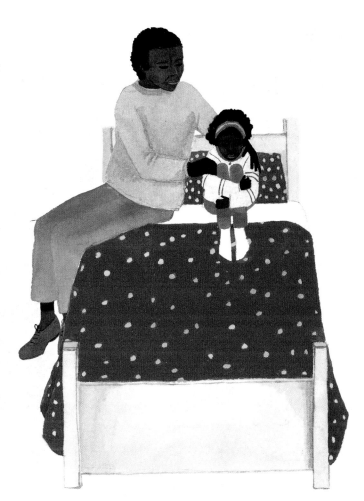

# My Father

My father doesn't live with us.
It doesn't help to make a fuss;
But I still feel unhappy, plus
   *I miss him.*

My father doesn't live with me.
He's got another family;
He moved away when I was three.
   *I miss him.*

I'm always happy on the day
He visits and we talk and play;
But after he has gone away
   *I miss him.*

*Mary Ann Hoberman*

# In Both the Families

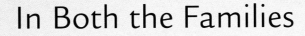
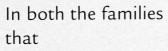

In both the families
that
    both belong to me,
there is every shade
of
brown, and tan,
and paler
        honey,
creamy gold.

I face faces that I see
in
    both the families
that
    both belong to me,
and
they can face
my crooked
      grin.

Here is every shade of every colour
                    skin.
    We fit in.

*Arnold Adoff*

# Mother Doesn't Want a Dog

Mother doesn't want a dog.
Mother says they smell,
And never sit when you say sit,
Or even when you yell.
And when you come home late at night
And there is ice and snow,
You have to go back outside because
The dumb dog has to go.

Mother doesn't want a dog.
Mother says they shed,
And always let the strangers in
And bark at friends instead,
And do disgraceful things on rugs,
And track mud on the floor,
And flop upon your bed at night
And snore their doggy snore.

Mother doesn't want a dog,
She's making a mistake.
Because, more than a dog, I think
She will not want this snake.

*Judith Viorst*

16

# Sauce

Aunt Ruth came from England
and guess all that we got
a jar of English mustard
which she said was very hot.

'That yellow thing no pepper!'
Remarked my aunty Dot.
'England famous for it strawberry
but for pepper it is not!'

Before we could prevent her
Aunt D dip in she big spoon.
It hot! It hot! So till
it nearly send her to the moon.

Now aunty Dot eats quietly
she scarcely speaks a word
she no touch the jar of mustard
since it deaden she taste-bud.

*Pauline Stewart*

# Our Baby

We've got a new baby
at our house

they call her Mandy Jane

she's fat and bald
with a line in charm
that's an absolute pain
when you've seen it all before

there's six of us now

so this new one's
got a lot of stick to come

but I reckon if anybody else
gets at her
he'd best know how to run

because
well

she's our kid sister
isn't she?

Joan Poulson

# Always Remembering Eloise

I felt her like a bag of tricks
One perfect somersaulting laugh
I marvelled as her tiny heart
Beat brightly on the photograph

I waited for her to appear
Part best-beloved, part enemy
Not of my flesh but of my blood
My baby sister yet to be

I never got to hear her cry
Or stick a plaster on her knee
Play scary monsters in the dark
Or beat her at Monopoly

Her absence feels solid as an oak
The 'might have beens' its fragile leaves
Which tumble gently to the ground
Always remembering Eloise.

*Lindsay MacRae*

# Sometimes

Sometimes I share things,
And everybody says
'Isn't it lovely? Isn't it fine?'

I give my little brother
Half my ice cream cone
And let him play
With toys that are mine.

But today
I don't feel like sharing.
Today
I want to be let alone.
Today
I don't want to give my little brother
A single thing except
A shove.

*Eve Merriam*

21

# The Runaway

I made peanut butter sandwiches.
I didn't leave a mess.
I packed my shell collection
and my velvet party dress,
the locket Grandma gave me
and two pairs of extra socks,
my brother's boy scout flashlight
and some magic wishing rocks.

Oh, they'll be so sorry.
Oh, they'll be so sad,
when they start to realise
what a nifty kid they had.

I'd really like to be here
when they wring their hands and say,
'We drove the poor child to it.
She finally ran away.'

If I peeked through the window
I'd see them dressed in black,
and hear them sob and softly sigh,
'Come back, dear child! Come back!'

The house will be so quiet.
My room will be so clean.
And they'll be oh so sorry
that they were oh so mean!

*Bobby Katz*

# Granny Granny
# Please Comb my Hair

Granny Granny please comb
my hair
you always take your time
you always take such care

You put me on a cushion
between your knees
you rub a little coconut oil
parting gentle as a breeze

Mummy Mummy
she's always in a hurry-hurry
rush
she pulls my hair
sometimes she tugs

But Granny
you have all the time
in the world
and when you're finished
you always turn my head and say
'Now who's a nice girl'

*Grace Nichols*

# Grandpa

Grandpa's hands are as rough as garden sacks
And warm as pockets.
His skin is crushed paper around his eyes
Wrapping up their secrets.

*Berlie Doherty*

# Let's Be Merry

Mother shake the cherry-tree,
　　Susan catch a cherry;
Oh how funny that will be,
　　Let's be merry!

One for brother, one for sister,
　　Two for mother more,
Six for father, hot and tired,
　　Knocking at the door.

*Christina Rossetti*

# Two Sisters

Two sisters, dressed in the threads of the universe, lived together
    in the sky, with only the sun and the moon for company.
To keep themselves amused, they danced on top of the rainbow.
    When they cried, it looked like dew. When they laughed,
Sunlight broke into pieces and covered the earth with turtledoves.

When the two sisters ran across the sky together, their footsteps
    echoed like thunder and woke the Creator from his nap.
He saw their beauty and turned them into morning stars. Now
    the two sisters greet the sun at dawn, making a path of splendour
Across the disappearing face of darkness in the sky.

*Nancy Wood*

# Grandad's Tree

We're planting a tree for my Grandad,
we've done it to help us recall
the hours he spent in the garden,
and the way that he thought of us all.

We didn't see Grandad too often,
he lived such a long way away,
and now that he's gone there are so many things
that I wish I had bothered to say.

But Mum says he knew that we loved him,
and how very much he loved us,
and he wouldn't have liked big, emotional scenes,
and he wouldn't have wanted a fuss;

So, we're planting a tree for my Grandad,
it's our way of saying Goodbye,
and its roots will reach down to the life-giving earth,
and its branches will stretch to the sky.

*Rowena Sommerville*

# Newcomers

My father came to England
from another country
my father's mother came to England
from another country
but my father's father
stayed behind.

So my dad had no dad here
and I never saw him at all.

One day in spring
some things arrived:
a few old papers,
a few old photos
and — oh yes —
a hulky bulky thick checkered jacket
that belonged to the man
I would have called 'Grandad'.
The Man Who Stayed Behind.
But I kept that jacket
and I wore it
and I wore it
and I wore it
till it wore right through
at the back.

*Michael Rosen*

# Family

There is only one man in the world
and his name is All Men.
There is only one woman in the world
and her name is All Women.
There is only one child in the world
and the Child's name is All Children.

*Carl Sandburg*

# ACKNOWLEDGEMENTS

'What is a Family?' from *Fathers, Mothers, Sisters, Brothers*, copyright © Mary Ann Hoberman 1991, published by Time Warner Books (formerly Little Brown & Co). 'Mom is Wow!' copyright © Julia Fields from *Families: Poems Celebrating the African American Experience*, complied by Dorothy S Strickland & Michael R Strickland 1994, published by Boyds Mills Press. 'Dad' from *Walking on Air*, copyright © Berlie Doherty 1993, published by HarperCollins. 'Mama' from *Coconut Kind of Day*, copyright © Lynn Joseph, published by Lothrop Lee & Shepherd. 'Missing Mama' from *Families*, copyright © Eloise Greenfield, published by Wordsong. 'My Father' from *Fathers, Mothers, Sisters, Brothers*, copyright © Mary Ann Hoberman 1991, published by Time Warner Books (formerly Little Brown & Co). 'In Both the Families' from *All the Colours of the Race*, copyright © Arnold Adoff 1992, published by HarperCollins and reproduced by their kind permission. 'Mother Doesn't Want a Dog' from *If I Were in Charge of the World and Other Worries*, copyright © Judith Viorst 1981, published by Simon & Schuster and reproduced with their kind permission. 'Sauce' from *Singing Down the Breadfruit*, copyright © Pauline Stewart, 1993, published by Bodley Head, a division of Random House. 'Our Baby' from *The Hutchinson Treasury of Children's Poetry*, copyright © Joan Poulson, published by The Random House Group. 'Always Remembering Eloise' from *How to Avoid Kissing Your Parents in Public*, copyright © Lindsay MacRae 2000, published by Penguin and reproduced by their kind permission. 'Sometimes' from *Catch a Little Rhyme*, copyright © Eve Merriam 1996, published by Simon & Schuster. 'The Runaway' from *The Random House Book of Poetry for Children*, copyright © Bobby Katz 1981, published by Random House Inc. 1983, also published as *The Walker Book of Poetry for Children*. 'Granny Granny  Please Comb My Hair' from *Come On Into My Tropical Garden*, copyright © Grace Nichols 1988, published by A&C Black Publishers Ltd. 'Grandpa' from *Walking on Air*, copyright © Berlie Doherty 1993, published by HarperCollins. 'Let's Be Merry' copyright © Christina Rossetti. 'Two Sisters' from *Dancing Moons*, copyright © Nancy Wood 1995, Bantam Doubleday Dell, published by Delacorte Press Books, Division of Random House Books, reproduced with the kind permission of Nancy Wood. 'Newcomers' from *Quick Let's Get Out of Here*, copyright © Michael Rosen 1983, published by Andre Deutsch. 'Grandad's Tree' from *The Martians Have Taken My Brother!*, copyright © Rowena Sommerville 1993, published by and reproduced with the kind permission of Hutchinson, a division of Random House. 'Family' copyright © Carl Sandburg from *Wheel Around the World* compiled by Chris Searle 1983, published by MacDonald.

The publishers have made every effort to contact holders of copyright material. If you have not yet received our correspondence, please contact us for inclusion in future editions.

# Barefoot Books
*Celebrating Art and Story*

At Barefoot Books, we celebrate art and story with books that open the hearts and minds of children from all walks of life, inspiring them to read deeper, search further, and explore their own creative gifts. Taking our inspiration from many different cultures, we focus on themes that encourage independence of spirit, enthusiasm for learning, and acceptance of other traditions. Thoughtfully prepared by writers, artists and storytellers from all over the world, our products combine the best of the present with the best of the past to educate our children as the caretakers of tomorrow.

www.barefootbooks.com